ALL OF THE FACTORS OF
WHY I LOVE
TRACTORS

WRITTEN BY
DAVINA BELL

ILLUSTRATED BY
JENNY LØVLIE

GREENWILLOW BOOKS, *An Imprint of* HarperCollins *Publishers*

All of the Factors of Why I Love Tractors
Text copyright © 2021 by Davina Bell
Illustrations copyright © 2021 by Jenny Løvlie

All rights reserved. Manufactured in Italy. For information address
HarperCollins Children's Books, a division of HarperCollins Publishers,
195 Broadway, New York, NY 10007.
www.harpercollinschildrens.com
The full-color art was created digitally. The text type is Gill Sans MT.

Library of Congress Cataloging-in-Publication Data

Names: Bell, Davina, author. | Løvlie, Jenny, illustrator.
Title: All of the factors of why I love tractors / written by Davina Bell ;
    illustrated by Jenny Løvlie.
Description: First edition. | New York, NY : Greenwillow Books, an Imprint
    of HarperCollins Publishers, [2021] | Audience: Ages 4–8. | Audience:
    Grades K–1. | Summary: Frankie McGee's mother takes him to the public
    library, where she tries to persuade him to choose a book about cars,
    helicopters, or anything else while he insists on yet another book about
    tractors.
Identifiers: LCCN 2020037445 | ISBN 9780063019188 (hardcover)
Subjects: CYAC: Stories in rhyme. | Tractors—Fiction. | Books and
    reading—Fiction. | Libraries—Fiction.
Classification: LCC PZ8.3.B3996 All 2021 | DDC [E]—dc23
    LC record available at https://lccn.loc.gov/2020037445

21 22 23 24 25 RTLO 10 9 8 7 6 5 4 3 2 1
First Edition

Greenwillow Books

For Ernie of Wills Domain, whose tractors
and kindness inspired this book ~ D. B.

For my dad, who gave me
my love of machinery ~ J. L.

I'm off on an outing with my mom today,
and we're not just going to the park to play.

Where are we going?

Can you guess?

Take a look!

(I'll give you a hint,

and the hint is

THIS BOOK!)

Down past the school and the pool and the shop,
I run through the door with a skip and a hop.

It's the library!

"Hello there, Frankie McGee,"
Miss Squid, the librarian, says to me.

"Oh, no!" says my mom with a very big groan,
when I show her the book that I want to take home.

"There are more than a million good books here to try!

Why is yours always about tractors, Frank,

WHY?"

"Oh, thank you for asking," I say with great glee.

"I'd love to explain why they're special to me

and tell you the many glorious factors

that go into the love that I have for all tractors."

"First . . ."

"The big strong treads on wheels that can travel
through huge muddy fields or across pits of gravel."

"A rumbling engine, a pipe that spits smoke,
a rake if you're raking, a hoe that can poke."

"A seat for the farmer,
a wheel that she steers,
a grumbling noise
as she changes gears."

"Levers and buttons
and pedals to press . . ."

"Trucks have those too!" my mom loudly protests.

"But Mom," I say. "Trucks just cannot do the things that a tractor can, let me tell you!"

"A tractor has different parts that attach—
a shovel for digging a vegetable patch,
a plow to turn earth so it's ready for seeds,
a sharp blade to chop all those troublesome weeds."

"Please stop!" says my mom.

"I have heard quite enough."

"But I'm only beginning—

they do even more stuff!"

"You used to like trains," my mother complains.

"But then I got bigger and so did my brain,
and I realized trains only chug down a track.
How boring—I'm snoring just thinking of that."

"Police cars have sirens!
Gliders have wings!"

"And forklifts have forks, if you're into those things.
But none of those is a good enough factor
to challenge my love for a shiny red tractor.
Like an old Massey Ferguson—what a machine!"

"Or if **red**'s not around, well, I guess I'll take green.

That's the color of tractors made by John Deere."

"I know," says my mom.

"I've been hearing all year.

What about . . ."

" . . . fire trucks with ladders and hoses?

Or planes, with their wide wings and cute little noses?

Cranes are so tall . . . they can help build a wall!

They can lift things up high, they deliver and haul.

A cement mixer?"

"All it does is go around."

"A steamroller?"

"It just sort of squashes the ground."

"What's wrong with tractors?
I don't understand."

"Oh, Frank, I'm sorry, but I just can't stand
any more books about them. Will these do instead?
Cable cars, submarines, taxis—a sled?
This one has rockets flying through space!
This one has cars driving fast in a race!"

"No, thanks," I say, in my most polite voice.

"But I think you'll be very pleased with my choice.

I'll lend it to you if you're interested, too.

There's a lot you could learn about what tractors do."

"FRANKIE!"

Mom hollers.

"Hush!"
says Miss Squid.
"Did you find
something, Frank?"

"Thank you! Yes, I did."

"For many various, glorious factors . . .

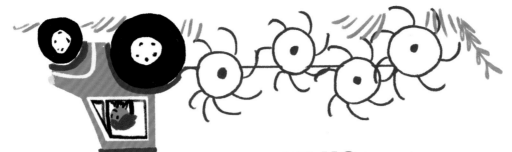

I want **THIS** book.

And it's all about tractors."

"What a surprise. I would never have guessed,"
says Miss Squid, with a wink. "Well, you know yourself best.
When you want something different, just come and find me.
A kid who likes books is a nice thing to see."

"Right, Mom?" I say, as we check my book out.

"I like books—that's what matters.

Not what they're about."

"And don't worry," I add.

"I know this one by heart.

I can read it to you—

when can we start?"